YAKS DON'T TALK
An Animal Name Game

Dedicated to my family

Special thanks to Aliye Çullu for graphic design assistance;
Valerie D'Ortona, creator of Isabel's World, for editorial assistance;
and Edmund Sypko, creator of Eurolingua® for permission
to use his "Pirate Eddy" character.

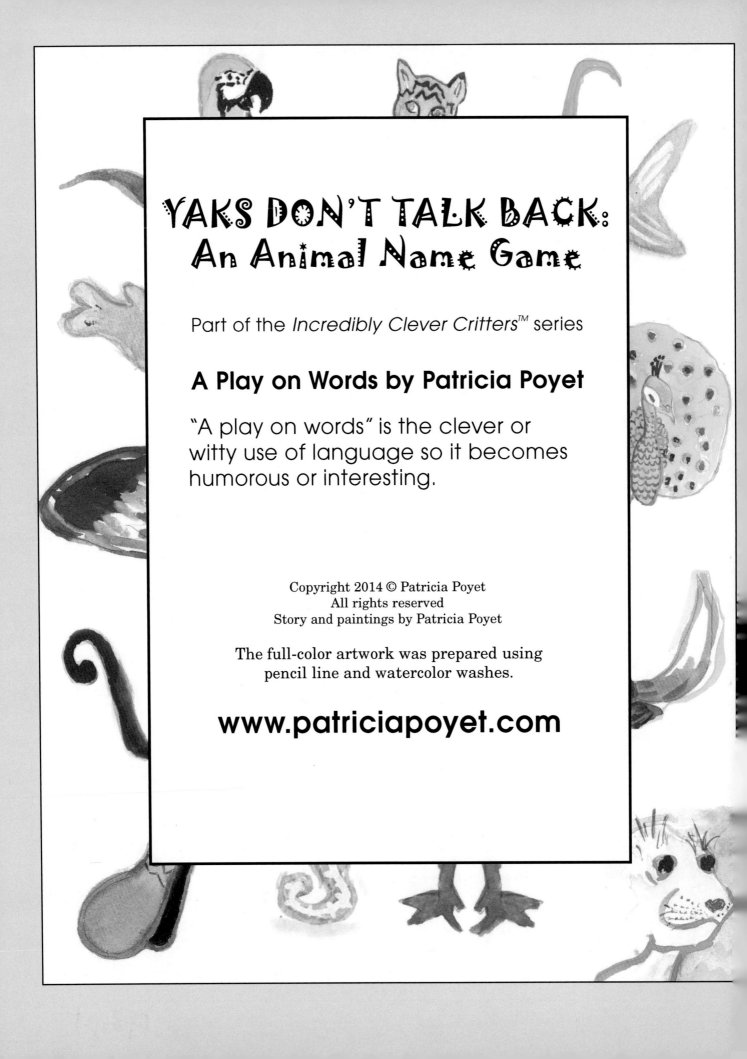

YAKS DON'T TALK BACK:
An Animal Name Game

Part of the *Incredibly Clever Critters*™ series

A Play on Words by Patricia Poyet

"A play on words" is the clever or witty use of language so it becomes humorous or interesting.

The full-color artwork was prepared using pencil line and watercolor washes.

www.patriciapoyet.com

Animals talk and squawk.
They twit and tweet.
They chat and chatter.
They meow and howl.
They quack and yak.
They grunt and bark.
They moo and coo.
Even their names say
and mean different things.

Read this book today,
and find out what animal
names can do and say.

An odd and squirrely tale began the day that Ava and her Nana spied a squirrel scampering up a tree. This particular critter carried a nut he intended to stash in his tree treasure chest. Nana quipped, "That squirrel is squirreling away his nut." Ava added, "And his doughnut."

Nana had a thought: animals that fly, swim, crawl, and run all have names that can be fun. If squirrels squirrel away, what can other animal names do and say? Clever critters create some amazing words.

So, a search was begun for more critter fun. A book called *Incredibly Clever Critters* was written with bats at bat, not so sheepish sheep, as well as starfish stars, and wormy bookworms.

However Ava has a little sister, and in a voice that was not a whisper, Celine said,

"Don't be mean. I need my turn.

I want to look for some words for a book."

Nana said, "I am sorry. Of course, we must take a look and write another book.

"Just like a ride on a merry-go-round, we will go look around for special animals with clever names in the sea and on the ground."

So Celine and her Nana went to search in all sorts of different spaces and places.

Let's read and see the animal names they found.

At the library, they took a look in an Audubon bird book. The spoonbill crane spoons up a marshy soup with his built-in spoon beak.

On February 2nd, in a small Pennsylvania town, they spied a shadow on the ground.
The groundhog hogs the spotlight on Groundhog's Day. When he sees his shadow on the ground, Celine and Nana know that winter will stick around, and snowmen and snowballs will not melt into the ground.

On a farm, they had some luck
and found a duck.
The daffy duck ducks down under
a pile of duck down and duck feathers.

On this farm, they found the last egg in a nest that was on a quest to become a chick. "Don't chicken out!" the chickens and other animals squawk to the egg as they are egging it on to hatch.

Crack out of your eggshell and make a peep.

While at a rodeo, Celine said, "Uh-oh!"
Celine and Nana had to watch out for some horns that were on the go.
Steer clear of this steer in case the cowboy loses his grip on his horn steering wheel.

At the beach they found a sight so sweet
it was not to be missed.
Celine and Nana gave their seal
of approval to two seals that sealed
their love with a kiss.

Away they snorkeled to search beneath the sea where rays of sunshine made the water sparkle. Stingrays with x-ray vision see through fish, a shark, a seahorse, and starfish with arms called rays.

POYET

In a garden in New Orleans, they found an assortment of cats including one who wore a hat. Imagine that!

Cool jazz cats play razzy, jazzy music while one cat catnaps. Catfish swim in a pond with cattails, and caterpillars munch and crunch on catalpa leaves.

POYET

On a treasure hunt they heard a parrot perform a stunt.
The parrot parrots what the pirate said and gives away the treasure chest's location. The parrot repeats...

At the zoo, Celine was hoping to chat with the yaks, but yaks don't say boo or moo or even coo. She didn't find yaks talking or yakking. She definitely didn't find yaks singing, "Yakkety Yak Don't Talk Back" because yaks don't talk back. From this herd of yaks, nothing was heard.

POYET

At a park on the 4th of July, Celine and Nana found a picnic spot where time flies by along with a fly and a butterfly.

They discover flies like to land on butter cream cupcakes, but butterflies prefer flowers the color of butter.

POKET.

While reading a fantasy tale about dragons, Celine and Nana found a dragon that was dragging along his tail and the end of this tale.

About the Author

Patricia Poyet is nuts about children's books. Her grandchildren enrich her life. She is the proud mother of four unique and wonderful individuals. Her children attribute much of their success to the countless books she read to them. She can trace her interest in children's books to her childhood experiences at the library. Characters such as Bemelmans' *Madeline*, Milne's *Winnie the Pooh* and M. Wise Brown's *Color Kittens Hush and Brush* led to her appreciation of both the visual arts and written word. She credits her mother for her introduction to the world of libraries and museums and her father for visits to the art supply store.

The inspiration for her critter books came from one of her granddaughters with whom she was squirrel watching. Other animals just kept joining in, and a book was born. Young children enjoy animals and word play. The author firmly believes that reading to children promotes success both academically and socially. She hopes you gather as many children as can fit in your lap to cuddle with, and ask the children questions as you read this book together.

Turn the page to play a fishing game. Find the animal words in this book on the fishes.

So keep on fishing for words.
They let you be heard.

Made in the USA
Columbia, SC
15 April 2017